Breakfast is Severed

A TyCobbsTeeth Thriller
by Robert Smith

Contents

"There are only nine meals between mankind and anarchy."

—*Alfred Henry Lewis*

Breakfast is Severed

His teeth broke through and sunk into its flesh. A hot, moist bouquet escaped and teased his nostrils—his euphoria was almost sexual. He bit down until his mouth watered. David Cameron's eyes rolled back in his head while he chewed that first bite of freshly toasted bagel.

Vibrations from his phone brought him around, breaking the trance aromas of coffee and bagel had pulled David into. He opened one eye and lifted the phone.

A message from his boss had come in. He tapped it with his thumb and groaned, "Not another pre-coffee crisis."

He licked cream cheese from the corner of his mouth and glanced at the clock on the stove. Thoughts of what he had yet to do raced through his mind.

Still in sweats from his run on the treadmill and needing to shower, David dumped the coffee he had just poured. He set his bagel down and turned to let his barking dog in.

The morning sky that had promised a clear sunny day just twenty minutes ago, was now black. Billowing charcoal plumes filled the air. The vast cornfield bordering his property blazed. Angry flames licking at his lawn like a red sea pounding against the shoreline.

Curly, his two-year-old labradoodle barked furiously at the fire for encroaching on his property.

David left the back door and crossed the lawn so fast his feet barely touched the grass. He scooped Curly up and headed top speed between the houses for the street.

David reached the sidewalk and heard sirens in the distance.

His sock feet, soaking wet from the dew, leaked out into puddles around his feet. He stood panting.

He looked down the row of houses to his right. The Bradley's house, six lots down, billowed black smoke. The Bradley family looked on in horror from the curb.

David put Curly in his car and scuttled across the lawn to the Able's house next door. He pounded on the door with one hand and rung the bell with the other. Then he ran to the next house, the Murphy's, before the Able had even answered.

Everyone else was already outside, but the Murphys and Able Kane were retired. David figured they were still in bed.

He reached the Murphy's door as the cry of the sirens neared. With a closed fist, he hammered.

Able Kane stepped out of the previous house David accosted. Able looked over. He held his housecoat together with one hand and tried to tame what was left of his thinning hair with the other.

"*What in Tarnation?*" he exclaimed before dashing back inside.

David heard movement. The door swung open and Andy Murphy presented David with a look of indignation.

The open door allowed a wave of sight and sound to wash over the old man. Emergency vehicles ripped past. The look of realization on his neighbor's face was all David needed; he was off and running back to grab his pooch.

Any thoughts David had of grabbing a few things from his house were dashed by the fire's progression. The red sea had crashed over the shoreline and washed against his house.

In his sock-feet, holding Curly in his arms, David stood across the street from his place. He realized this was the last time he would be looking at the home where he grew up.

David watched helplessly while the flames moved methodically from the back of the house to the side. They nibbled away at the bottom edge of the siding the same way he ate the edge off his Oreos.

He noticed an orange glow inside the main floor windows and then the drapes disappeared unceremoniously. The fire drew his attention back to the side of the house as it became impatient with nibbling and decided to devour the rest of the side at once. The flames quickly ate their way up through the soffit and into the attic.

Moments later the whole house erupted into a fireball. Some structural shifting made the dog flinch in his arms. A window shattered and Curly to jumped.

David felt like he had run ten miles in full combat gear carrying a fifty-pound rucksack. He felt gravity pulling down on him. A vice compressed his chest and spots were jumping around in front of his eyes.

David shook his head, blinked his eyes, and focused on the new noise disturbing the airwaves.

"I need everyone to clear the area, now! We are clearing a five-block radius—immediately!"

The blaring megaphone voice, although startling, brought lucidity. People—most of them his neighbors—moved past him toward the corner of the block.

"David, are you okay?" Andy Murphy asked. "C'mon, we've got to go." His neighbor walked past with a box of granola bars in one hand and a carton of orange juice in the other.

David fell into formation behind the large exodus. He realized his boss was still waiting for a response.

The weight of the twenty-five-pound dog caused his arms to ache. Finally, Curly's sharp elbows forced David to set her down.

"Curly, come," he commanded and again started towards the corner.

He pulled his phone from his pocket and dialed. After three rings, someone answered.

"Telecom Ops Chief Richards will have to call you back."

"What? Wait!" David quipped. "He's too busy to answer his own phone?"

"David, he's meeting with the Comms unit and ordering field kits to be prepped and loaded A.S.A.P."

"What? What's going on Peg?"

"Shit's hittin' the fan. You haven't seen the news?"

"Peg, my house just burned down. I'm out on the street... being ordered to get off the street."

"Oh David, I feel for you, I do. Listen, though, you've got to get your skinny butt in here—like fifteen minutes ago."

"Roger that, Peg; I'll be there in T-minus fifteen." He hung up and pocketed his phone.

Comms units? Why the hell is Doug prepping communications units and field kits? David wondered. He must be setting up command control communications someplace. Why. What the hell is going down?

David, an Information Technology Specialist for the Army's 7th Signal Command reported to Chief, Doug Richards.

His chief was responsible for all base systems and communications as well as support for all domestic Army units from corps to battalion.

Under Chief Richards's command, David's mandate was to ensure all computer networks and systems on the base purred like kittens. He normally ran everything from his office and did so with effectiveness and efficiency.

"C'mon Curly, let's go. *Double-time.*"

David picked up his sock feet, broke into a jog and led his pup around the corner. They headed up the hill, weaving through bodies until they got to the top of Maple Hill Drive.

Maple Hill intersected with Truman Boulevard five blocks from his house, the location of the closest bus stop.

Glancing back down the hill, David watched his neighbors plodding their way. He took a seat, pulled out his phone and called Jessie's cell phone.

He had been seeing Jessie for six months, which was the longest relationship he had had—besides Curly. David was twenty and Jessie was twelve years older than that. The guys at work bugged him about having a mommy fetish. Who knows, maybe there was something to that since he hooked up with her a year after his mom died, but he didn't care, he loved Jessie.

He met her at the dog park. She was out walking her pooch, Frank, a female miniature dachshund. Their dogs played and they talked. Her perfume intoxicated him, but it was her sense of humor that really hooked David.

"David? Where are you? Are you okay?"

"Yeah babe, I'm good. We're good. I've got Curly with me up on Truman. There was a fire."

"I know," Jessie interrupted. "I just heard it on the news. I'm on my way over."

For the first time since he'd met her, David read panic in Jessie's voice.

David stood up; Jessie didn't live far. He looked north on Truman and saw her car rounding the bend.

She drove and spoke, her eyes wild. David had not seen the morning news and a lot had happened. He listened to Jessie and his head swiveled as they drove.

In driveways, people loaded their cars. On the roads, people drove recklessly—more so than usual. Traffic was heavy and sirens sounded from every direction.

The surroundings gave credibility to his girlfriend's crazy stories.

They cleared the base gates and pulled up outside David's building.

Jessie said she would head back to her place to get Frank. She would load the car with provisions, ready their two pooches, and await his call.

"You've got two hours to fix your bosses problem and give me a call. That's eleven-hundred-hours your time, soldier," she said with a thin smile. "I'll be waiting."

He got out of the car, turned back and leaned in. "Thanks babe. I'll call as soon as I can."

"Love you," she said.

David forced his stressed face into a smile. "Love you too."

David walked into Chief Richards' outer office where the Chief's assistant, Peg, was on the phone. She looked frazzled. Peg glanced up and waved him in but kept the receiver pressed to her head.

Chief Richards looked up from some papers on his desk and his eyebrows popped. His eyes scanned David up and down. "You had better rectify your aesthetics, soldier. I need you in a uniform—*A-SAP!*"

"Sir, I..."

"Listen David, I got a call at zero-dark-thirty by a lieutenant ordering me to a meeting when I should have been horizontal for another four hours. I've been here for seven hours already and you stroll in wearing *mufti? — and no shoes?*"

"Sir, my uniforms burned with my house this morning. I had to bum a drive to get here."

"*I don't give a...* Oh." Hi boss's demeanor softened. "Well... find yourself one and be in the conference room at oh-nine-hundred—*sharp.*"

"Yes sir."

David walked into the conference room a few minutes early. Lieutenant-Colonel Greg Jeffreys and Captain Peter Moore sat at the far end of a long table, involved in a heated exchange.

"Sirs."

The two men glanced over and acknowledged him, "Specialist Cameron, please take a seat," said Jeffreys.

David parked himself midway down the row of seats. Jeffreys continued.

"That was a load of crap, Peter. There was no hit on the POTUS motorcade."

"Yeah, I wasn't convinced there was, but even so," started Captain Moore. "Things are escalating. Food riots broke out in Britain last week, just days after the news of their shortage was leaked."

Moore's eyes widened as he spoke.

"In Japan, riots started in two days—total chaos in four. Hell, one week after their market dried up, we heard reports of cannibalism."

Captain Moore's already wide eyes, stretched further as he leaned in.

"Cannibalism, Greg. And now the Netherlands have lost complete control. There's been no word out of The Hague in two days."

With a dismissive hand gesture, Jeffreys responded, "You're talking apples and oranges, Peter. Those countries couldn't feed their populations before the crisis started. They were getting by on imports. With no imports—they were done." He shrugged his shoulders and kept going. "Look at Germany. They released info to their people stating figures and timelines. They managed to maintain order by communicating and setting up a ration distribution system. They're still solid," he said, holding up a clinched a fist.

David only half-listened as they spoke. For the most part, they had been replaying highlights from the past week's news. He had another concern.

There were plenty of reasons why such a high-level emergency meeting would have been called. David mulled thoughts on why he, a low-level grunt would be there.

Moore sat back in his chair, his eyes still bugging out.

"I dunno, Greg. I look at places like Panama and Costa Rica that have gone black. And the mayhem in Guatemala... the riots in Mexico. They're right in our backyard."

"Peter, calm the fuck down," Jeffreys barked. His brow lowered.

Peter Moore's eyes flitted to David. David looked down at the table.

"You're being paranoid," continued Jeffreys. "There's gonna be casualties, we knew that. And more countries are going to implode. There are another sixty countries that couldn't feed themselves before this started."

He threw his hands up and leaned back in his chair. "Face it," he continued. "They're not gonna make it either. That's why we pulled everyone from those embassies last week."

"I don't know if I'm being paranoid," mumbled Captain Moore. "From what I heard this morning, we've got rowdy crowds from Maryland to Massachusetts—and they're getting ugly. Riots have started here. Things are about to simmer over."

Moore's last words peaked David's attention.

"Okay, now you're being naïve," replied Jeffreys. "Look—FEMA is already set up. We just need to get those crowds herded into the camps. We will maintain control."

What? David's eyes widened. Oh, my God. It's here. It's started.

The room darkened. David Cameron's eyes darted to the doorway. An imposing figure entered, several high-level lackies at his heel.

"Let's get started." boomed Lieutenant-General Wayne Scantley.

Lieutenant-General Scantley, Colonel Moss, and Major Riggs grabbed seats at the head. Chief Richards entered, closed the door, and found a seat.

"Colonel Moss, bring us up to speed on the new National Emergency Operations Center (NEOC)," instructed Scantley.

"Sir, the NEOC at Fort New Dawn was brought online nine days ago. It's been operational for the last seven days. All testing and initial operations have been successful. They're ready for our delta migration and cutover."

Lieutenant Colonel Greg Jeffreys spoke up. "Everything is a go?"

"Affirmative. Cyber Command's servers are installed; data synchronization began seventy-two hours ago. Everything else is a go—the rest of the cooks are in the kitchen."

David felt like he walked through a door into the twilight zone. Cooks are in the kitchen? What the hell is this guy talking about? Migrating Cyber Command?

Although David was involved with preparations for a backup site, he was told it was contingency planning. The emergency offsite backup was supposed to get funded *next* fiscal.

"Doug," the Colonel started. "How much time to complete your piece?"

Chief Richards looked at David. "How long to copy over the deltas and confirm Specialist?"

David stood up. "Sir, I need to stop all services and snapshot the deltas. Transfer could take up to sixty minutes. Testing will take about fifteen minutes—once the transfer finishes."

Lieutenant General Scantley rose. "Well, we better wrap this up so you can get started, son."

They all stood.

Scantley continued. "We're stopping at Fort Leonard Wood to join up with the 94th Engineer Battalions and the 92nd Military Police Battalion. They will be accompanying us to Fort New Dawn."

David's mind flashed, Fort New Dawn? If that's the backup site, it's in Illinois. Jesus—what about Jessie?

The general's gaze moved from man to man. "You have exactly three hours to pack your kits, kiss your wives and have your butts on the trucks. I want wheels on the road at twelve-hundred-hours."

David walked out of the conference room reeling from what he'd heard. *Time is ticking,* he realized. The general expected him to finish his piece in the next ninety minutes. If he started now, he could talk to Jessie during the transfer. David leaned into a jog.

"David wait."

Chief Richards caught up to him and apologized for not having had time to bring him up to speed before the meeting. The news flooded in all night.

Fires in Nebraska spread west into Colorado and east into Kansas. Crops and livestock were destroyed across three states. Information about the food shortages leaked and violence broke out all over the country.

Chief Richards did not realize that David had stopped walking three steps before.

"David?" he asked, looking back to find him standing with eyes wide.

"I... I've got to call Jessie!"

David pulled out his cell phone and held J. It didn't ring. He pulled it from his ear and looked at the screen. "Damn—no service."

"David, there's more." Chief Richards continued.

"Some of the 'operations' being run by the 'other cooks' in Fort New Dawn include cellular jamming."

"What the hell?"

"Yeah. They tell me that they started jamming this morning. It's one of the emergency protocols. All civilian communications will be cut-off until we get a handle on things."

Chief Richards saw the look of desperation on David's face.

"Look, David. Get that transfer started and then take my car over to say goodbye to Jessie."

"Really, Sir? I appreciate it, thanks. What about Donna?"

"We're old fashioned," he answered with a smile. "We still have a landline. I'm on my way to my office to bring her up to speed right now."

Chief Richards winked and walked off.

David started the transfer and then ran—full out—all the way to the parking lot. He wheeled out of the lot and weaved in and out of the heavy traffic.

Images of Curly greeting him at the door—tail wagging—entered his head. He imagined Jessie's tight embrace, her warm cheek, and that amazing fragrance.

Desperate drivers kept David sharp as he made his way to Jessie's street. The fifteen-minute drive took less than ten before he pulled into her driveway.

With eagerness and a little trepidation, David shifted the car into park and shut the engine off.

Jessie's front door hung ajar. David's excitement ebbed—*apprehension rose.*

Jessie car was in the driveway. She was not in her yard. David saw no movement in the front windows, or any reason for the open door.

Scanning the area, he saw a jam-packed car across the street. It looked ready for a long trip. The neighbor, Ted, came out the front door carrying a box. He nodded. Two houses to the left, neighbors were loading up their RV. Other than that, the street was quiet.

David jumped out of the car and ran to the partially open door. He eased it open and leaned in. Nothing in the entrance or front room seemed out of place. He heard noise coming from the kitchen.

Adrenaline coursed through him. Anxiety eased and excitement began to build.

It's Jesse. An uncertain smile played on his lips. *She's packing supplies.*

He approached the kitchen entrance, warning signs struck him. Everything was wrong. Cans and broken glass were strewn about the floor. An odd sound came from the far side of the kitchen. He couldn't place it. He did not look there; something kept his eyes on the floor.

The human brain gathers input from all senses unconsciously. It processes and deduces. This is instinct. Yet, it will try to find hope, as that is our nature.

David's mind offered up suggestions, *scenarios*. He sifted through them as he crept toward the corner.

There's a thief—a looter. He's rummaging—that's the noise. Jessie is hiding with the dogs—they're safe.

Jesse is hiding—*yes*—he wanted to believe this, but inevitably, his mind wrestled with it. The unusual noise was not *rummaging*. He knew he had heard these sounds. He had smelled the coppery odor, before. But he dismissed it. He knew the dogs would not hide quietly with someone in the house.

His eyes moved over the broken glass. Shattering sounds, heavy thumping noises from cans hitting the floor. Frank could not have sat in silence while someone ransacked the place.

That familiar noise… that smell—he dismissed them again and slunk forward, eyes low.

One more hesitant step brought reality to bare everything into view.

Just inside the door lay Frank. The little dog on her side—motionless. His heart sank to his stomach.

David's eyes moved from Frank. They crossed the floor to another fallen object. He felt weak. His stomach bucked like it was going to puke. David put his hand to his mouth and swallowed hard.

David saw legs. Jessie's legs. She lay prone on the cold tile floor. He couldn't see the rest of her from his side of the table, but he saw blood. He saw a lot of blood.

Adrenaline worked its magic again. This time, it wasn't light-hearted excitement—*eagerness*. This time, his blood ran hot, his body stiffened, his fists balled up. Fury gripped him.

David's eyes swept across the floor to the matt in front of the sink. His eyes widened with a focus only rage can bring.

A pool of blood soaked the matt. It encircled the legs that stood at sink. He scanned up the legs to the counter. His pup, Curly lay atop, partially blocked by the figure.

The rage that brought sharpness to his vision and white-knuckled strength to his grip, also fogged his mind.

The surreal scene left David's head swimming. He felt like he was dreaming, or watching it on some gruesome late-night television show.

Curly's head lay, mouth open and tongue on the counter. His head was jerking, as if someone was tugging on him. *Blip, blip, blip* drew David's attention to the figure's right. Blood dripped from a coil of bowels.

He looked away from his pet. The man at the sink became the sole focus of his attention.

David's burning eyes, strained to focus through tears that had welled up. His brow lowered. Its weight narrow his eyes into angry slits. Tears had started to stream down his face.

The psychopath stood at the counter with his back to David. His long hair looked wild, tangled, and soiled with dry blood. He stopped his work and lowered a knife to his side.

Turning slowly and lowering his stance into a crouch, the blood-covered maniac looked like an animal about to pounce. A smile stretched across his face. "A man's gotta eat," he said in a low-pitched growl.

He tilted his head to the side then leapt forward. The knife came at David in a high, wide arc from the left.

David responding instinctively. Years of hand-to-hand combat training kicked in.

David planted his back foot and leaned forward. He thrust his hands out together, elbows wide. His left forearm met the inside of the maniac's arm. David's right elbow crashed into the man's jaw. Immediately, David hooked his hands onto the back of the man's shoulder and neck. He grabbed on tight. He yanked the man forward and brought his knee up.

The blow struck the killer's midsection bending him further. The knife clattered to the floor, but David kept throwing knees. The third knee-strike landed and the wind come out of the man. David felt him go limp.

Twisting hard and fast, David brought his left elbow around. It landed on the slumped man's jaw with a sickening *CRACK*. The psycho's face slammed into the floor. He lay motionless.

David reached for his phone to dial 911. Dead air reminded him the service was down.

With a shaky—adrenaline-drunk—hand, he tried to push the phone back into his pocket. It slipped and clunked to the floor.

"Damn it."

David bent to grab it. He sensed a presence entering the room. From his crouch, he glanced up. The butt of a rifle swooped down for a kiss. All went black.

Bumping and jostling brought David around.

"I see sleeping beauty is awake," said a loud voice.

He squinted to see a man sitting across from him. He was bouncing up and down on his bench and smiling at David. There were others beside him that came into focus. Soldiers. He was in the back of a truck full of soldiers and gear.

"How the—" he managed, as the man beside him put his hand on David's shoulder. "Relax man," he said. "You've been through an ordeal."

"Alex? How did I get here?"

"We were getting ready to pull out and there was still no sign of you. Peg came running from the office. She received a call from Jessie's neighbor, Ted.

"Ahh, Ted."

"So, we hauled butt over and found you, bud."

David reached for his temple and winced.

"You're lucky that neighbor saw. Even luckier he had the balls to go in and scare the crazy bitch off."

David put his hands to his head and squeezed to ease the pain and keep his head from splitting open.

The memories of what he had seen—what had happened, flashed through his memory like a horrible slide show. He leaned forward with his head in his hands.

After what seemed like days of driving, word came back from the front, "We're entering the burn zone."

David tilted his head toward Alex, "Burn zone?"

"Yeah, that's what they're calling the area behind the wildfire line. It's quarantined. They have a line drawn from Utah to Kentucky and up to Lake Michigan. The Midwest is a dead zone."

The truck slowed and then stopped for several minutes. He heard many voices up ahead. It sounded like distant yelling.

Eventually, they lurched forward and started moving again. As they bounced and bumped, the voices became louder. It became clear enough to identify. David heard the indistinct mutterings of an unhappy crowd.

Through the opening at the back of the truck, David saw they were passing through a crowd of people. The people were hungry. They wanted food and water. Some pleaded; many demanded.

The truck passed through rows of soldiers behind sandbag walls and past several gates. He watched, as soldiers would hurry to close each gate as they passed.

Twenty minutes later, the trucks pulled into Fort Leonard Wood. David looked down at his watch. Sure enough, it was twenty-two-hundred-hours.

They had enough time to hit the mess hall and the latrine before the Engineer Battalions finished packing their trucks.

Word was the Military Police Battalion had pulled out an hour earlier. They were called up to bolster defenses at the St. Louis checkpoint. There was a situation in need of defusing.

The pale orb overhead glowed through thin cloud cover. And before the clock hit twelve, the convoy had been readied.

A heavy-hearted David Cameron pulled himself up onto the truck, dropped his rucksack. He plunked down and the tailgate slammed shut.

The last vehicle departed Fort Leonard Wood before zero-dark-thirty.

They were on their way to Fort New-Dawn, Illinois.

Specialist Hubbard, sitting beside David, hauled his field radio up onto his lap. He snapped it on and started tuning, working from four hundred and down.

Chatter across that he tried to hone in on. He worked the knob until the voices became clearer.

"It's St Louis, guys," he announced. "The checkpoint is under duress. I'm picking up chatter from the 92nd."

Sergeant Green stood up and leaned in to hear, "Yeah, that's the Military Police Battalion from Fort Leonard Wood."

Hubbard agreed, "Yup, they headed to St. Louis just before we got to the fort. We're only about five minutes out now."

"Jesus," Green said. "It sounds like we might be in for some action."

Indications from the conversation on the radio were that violence was escalating. The crowd was throwing rocks and pushing back on the fencing.

A beating sound from a helicopter closed in. The canopy over their heads started to rattle from heavy wind.

"Jeez, that's low," exclaimed Hubbard.

"Yup." replied Green. "Sounds like an Apache. I'd bet it's an AH-64E Apache Guardian."

The driver yelled back that they were being ordered to detour around the checkpoint.

"Strap yourselves down, guys. Sounds like things are gonna be rough ahead."

To David, it sounded like the irate fans at the last game of his high school football career. Those were sounds he would never forget.

There were more than thirty-thousand on hand to see them be crushed by their archrivals that night. Thirty-thousand surrounded them, yelled, and threatened them.

The unruly mob threw whatever they could find onto the field.

As David and his team huddled up to call their last play, a shoe actually hit the guy next to him.

The here-and-now slapped David across the face jolting him out of his daydream. A rock the size of a baseball, hit the floor in front of him. The rock bounced up and hit Sergeant Green.

"You bastards," Green hissed. He pulled the rifle off his shoulder and readied it.

The truck's canopy came to life as objects started pounding it from the outside.

Several gunshots registered close by; the shots frenzied the crowd. Through the small opening at the back of the truck, a mob began swarming.

The brakes engaged and no one was ready. David fell hard into the aisle. Bodies toppled over him.

He struggled to untangle himself from the pile of people and regain his feet. Chaos had now begun in the back of their truck.

Angry faces screamed in through back of the truck as they regained their feet.

Sergeant Green ran to the back as someone tried to climb in. He struck the invader in the face with his boot. Green pulled his foot back. He lined up to stomp another, but hands grabbed hold. An octopus of arms sprang up from behind the truck's tailgate and pulled Sergeant Green off balance. He tried to grab the edge of the canopy with his outstretched hand, but missed. He fell outward with a look of terror on his face.

A heavy rain of feet, rocks and makeshift weapons stomped out Green's pleas.

Hubbard, who was closest to the back, sat stunned. Two soldiers quickly knocked Hubbard to the floor, pushing past to secure the back.

David hunted for his weapon. Others did the same. Then a hail of automatic gunfire erupted. Heads whipped around to find the two soldiers standing at the truck's tailgate. Horror struck David. He thought they had attacked the people. The two soldiers had their weapons readied, but the rain of bullets didn't come from them.

Above all other noise, screams ripped through the air. The horror of bloodshed tore through the crowd. A deafening, single shot echoed through the truck. One of the soldiers staggered back from the tailgate. He fell to his knees clutching his stomach.

The other tailgate-guard stepped forward. He squeezed the trigger of his rifle and began screaming. He strafed back and forth, and he screamed.

A final bullet left the chamber of his rifle. The weapon exhausted its clip. The last few brass shell casings chimed on the floor. The scream faded with his breath and his expression of anger morphed to horror.

He dropped his weapon and stumbled backwards into the truck, then fell to his butt.

Time stood still.

Everyone in the truck stared toward the opening at the back.

Although the crowd could still be heard like a roaring ocean in the distance, a quiet fell over the small area behind them.

"You mother fuckers!" was the first noise to shatter the stillness of shock. The painful sound of anguish followed—crying, and wailing, and screaming.

Their truck lurched forward and started moving again. David walked wearily to the back.

He grasped both sides of the partially open canopy and leaned outward. He watched as they pulled away from the gruesome scene. The screams of pain and loss faded as the truck moved on.

They passed through the outer edge of the crowd and onto clearer streets. David saw the looks of desperation, not anger or malice.

To David the single-word signs, carried by some, along the side of the road spoke volumes. These were people in need of food and water. They sought means of taking care of their families. They were desperate.

He remembered hearing someone say something years before. It resonated with him.

"We are only nine meals from anarchy".

That prophecy was now coming to be, he thought.

A figure caught David's attention. One boy, about twelve, stood alone at the side of the road. He wore soiled blue jeans and a tattered t-shirt. The boy's head followed David as they drove past. His eyes fixed on David's. He held a sign that read,

WHAT'S FOR SUPPER?

"Fort New Dawn," barked a voice from the front. "—thirty minutes out."

David watched from the opening at the back of the truck, while the cityscape disappeared into darkness.

Epilogue

This story was inspired by the prevailing premise that society is only three meals from anarchy.

If you found this story appetizing and would like to follow up with the entrée, you can continue reading with the novel, *Society for Supper*.

Society for Supper takes you through the thunderstorm of collapsing society as a member of the Donnelly family (*a parallel storyline*).

SOCIETY for SUPPER
Book 1 in the Series: 9 Meals
A TyCobbsTeeth Thriller by Robert Smith

Ben Donnelly just got his life back together. Now, the world around him is falling apart.

A drought swept across the planet causing food shortages worldwide. Its effects crept across the planet for weeks. Riots broke out and violence ensued, but that was only the beginning.

Chaos began to tear away at the very fabric of society. Americans sat back and watched as civilians around the world descended into darkness. Their government told them they were safe—insulated, as the rest of the world was pulled into the quickening spiral.

The Donnelly family finds catastrophic events have now reached their quiet neighborhood. America too is being sucked into the vortex—terror has found them. Their life and everything around them is about to be torn apart.

Ben Donnelly, a former S.W.A.T. officer with the Boston police force, is in the fight of his life and will do anything to protect his family from the storm of inhumanity.

About the Author

Robert Smith, the author of What Lies Within, lives in Ontario, Canada with his wife Rhonda, their Tibetan-terrier, Cheeky-Monkey, and their two daughters, Shelby and Jordan.

www.robertsmiththrillers.ca

Printed in Great Britain
by Amazon

21244193R20020